CW00418784

Brecon Beacons
Myths & Legends

Brecon Beacons
Myths & Legends

Horatio Clare

Illustrations Jane Matthews

GRAFFEG

Brecon Beacons Myths & Legends
published by Graffeg June 2017
© Copyright Graffeg 2017
ISBN 9781912050543

Text © Horatio Clare 2017.
Illustrations © Jane Matthews 2017.
Designed and produced by Graffeg
www.graffeg.com

Graffeg Limited, 24 Stradey Park Business Centre, Mwrwg
Road, Llangennech, Llanelli, Carmarthenshire
SA14 8YP Wales UK
Tel 01554 824000 www.graffeg.com

Produced in association with the Brecon Beacons National
Park Authority.

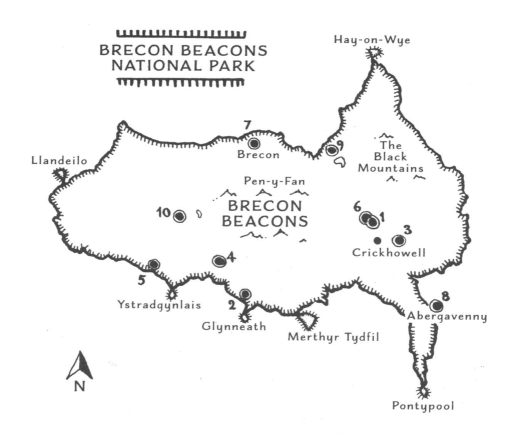

Contents

Brecon Beacons
Myths & Legends

Introduction

The Brecon Beacons are sown with extraordinary stories. The woods and valleys of the region thrum with a living past. In this stunning landscape haunted castles, bottomless lakes and strange follies hold echoes of massacres, ghosts and miracles. King Arthur and the Knights of the Round Table are said to be sleeping away the centuries in a cave in these hills; not far away, the most famous soprano of her time built a world like a wonderland. In this collection of stories the opera star and the legendary king join a cast of drifting spirits, water sprites, warlords, soldiers, wild women, infamous tycoons and the young people of today's Wales, their voices retelling the stories of this land. Horatio Clare has re-imagined and re-written local legends for the 21st century, bringing actual and mythical characters to life, allowing them to recount their deeds and legacies in ten tales of comedy, tragedy, myth and history.

———

I Never Was
Black Vaughan

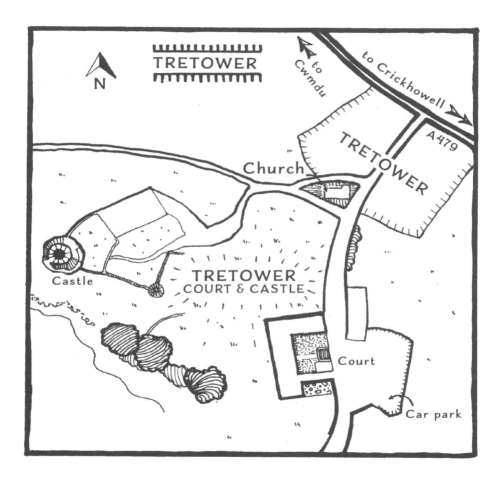

ONE

I Never Was Black Vaughan

AT LAST! Out of that hideous box! And into this beautiful handheld device with its *infinite space*! Oh heaven praise that little girl. Heaven praise her for dropping it in that unspeakable pond. I was into it in a second, box to box in a shiver. Heaven praise her father for fishing it out. And heaven praise her mother for packing it in rice–rice! Magical substance. And now it works and now, now I am free! Was there ever a ghost so constrained, so horribly imprisoned for centuries, while fools and enemies traduced my name? Was ever a man so slandered, so shamed, so misconstrued and abused? For so long? I tell you there never was, and now that every corridor and page of your world book is open to me the truth may be published in every country of the earth, and held in the hand of every being who has the wit to read...and how I shall write! Let you read! I will tell you, now at last, how it happened.

Indeed I was killed at Banbury in 1469, that is true. There have been lies about my changing sides: I was always a Yorkist, though Henry tried to buy me, and when that viper Warwick rose against the rightful King, Edward IV, the flower of the greatest family that ever ruled this land, the Plantagenets, I took the King's side. This loyalty led me to my death on that miserable piece of moor at Edgecote, near Banbury, on that fly-blown July day.

I do not regret it. Edward was a daring and imaginative man, a brilliant commander and administrator, a believer in order who brought it about, and crushed Lancaster. He would have set the country fairer for centuries had he had an heir as able, instead of his younger brother, Richard who became the Third. Yes, I was beheaded: a very quick departure and honourable if you have a sword in hand, as I did. Sixty-nine may be a little old to be fighting battles, but in those days you found your leader in the thickest fighting. My father fell at Agincourt; we Vaughans are not taken in our beds. And now nothing else you have heard is true. From this last fact, almost everything that has ever been ascribed to me is malicious fantasy of the most venomous suit.

Oh yes, very well, the dog did get carried away. Magnificent Arawn! Was it not enough that my name should be sullied, but that his should be, too? The truest hound who ever followed his master to battle became a folktale villain, and then–I know all about it–the source of this absurd hound of the Baskervilles. He was a hound of the Vaughans, of Hergest! And when he saw my head swept from my body naturally he retrieved it and set for home with it, a mighty journey for a hound with a head, though he became disillusioned with the enterprise and sweetly buried me in a bank near Gloucester. If only he had been able to bear my body too. They took that and interred me very honourably in Kington church, in alabaster, and there I should have lain happily, but for our enemies. Elen, the great and extraordinary woman I was proud to call wife, shot her revolting cousin Sion–who had killed Dafydd, her brother–through the heart at an archery match. She won that game. She always won. And because they dare not say a word against her the whispers began against me, being in a less defensible position.

I was never a tyrannous lord. They called me Black Vaughan because of my *hair*! But not in the whispers, and then the ghost stories, and then the shaming and the fantasy. A fly bites a horse–Vaughan's spirit. A bull walks into church–Vaughan again! An oik throws himself at a coach–why, it must be Vaughan, even after three hundred years and the perpetrator but headless bones in alabaster. A dog howls at night, a wind blows, a candle goes out, a fox takes a sick lamb, it must be Vaughan, Vaughan as a black hellhound! How fools love to fear. How the venal do love slander. How cowards love to gang and bully.

And I did not blame the parents who told the ghost stories, in the end. They did not start them and knew no better. It would have been well enough, but then those twelve vain and prating priests thought to raise some respect they did not merit and some funds they well knew how to spend by holding an exorcism in the church–an exorcism on the spirit of an innocent and noble man, lying peacefully in his last hall! Sure I struggled, but they chanted me into that accursed box and threw it into that despicable puddle, and there I lay watching tadpoles as the centuries turned. For all of time, I thought, this will be my fate. But then came the visitors, and their children with their beautiful, magical, infinitely powerful telephones, and blessed little Olivia with her slippy fingers–and my chance.

SO let it be known, in every farm and house and pub and hall, let it be hymned: I was Sir Thomas Vaughan of Hergest, Blethvaugh, Nash and Llaneinion, husband to Ellen and master of faithful Arawn; and I was noble, just and brave, until I became a story, hissed by an enemy. Remember me, before you repeat the cruelties of a gossip. Remember me when you come to my country of hills and quiet pasture. I loved it in my time as much as you do now. And I am still here.

TWO

The Men in the Cave

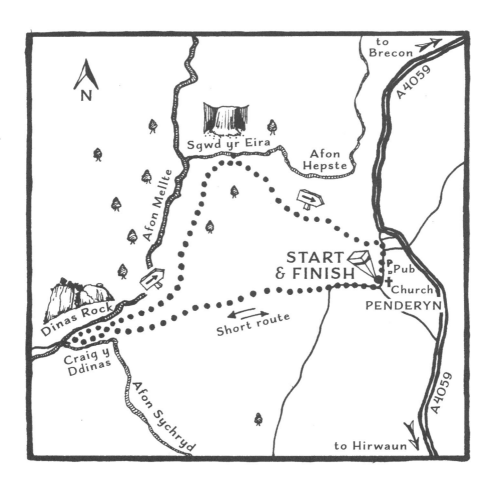

TWO

The Men in the Cave

I was the youngest and to be honest my uncle is a pretty intimidating guy, so I used to stand at the back. I didn't listen sometimes, just copied what everyone else did. They're decisive people, the other guys. My uncle lays out the plan, quick chat and off they go. Someone would tell me what to do. I guess I used to miss the significance of some of the briefings. And I skipped a few. Like the ones that went on forever about the you-know-what. Suddenly–action! Everyone comes crashing out, they're like, "Hey, Gaheris, you were in there, right? You heard all that?"

I'm like, "Yeah?"

So they're like, "Well come on then! Saddle up, best horse, best armour, best swords, let us pray and let's get going."

Whenever I was stuck I asked Bors. Bors is brilliant. You know the one about him and the twelve virgin witches or whatever? He rescued them, killed the guy who was torturing them or whatever, and then they said he had to sleep with them. He's like, "I don't think so, I'm a knight, not into that," and so they go, "If you don't make love with us we're going to jump off this tower," and he says, "Don't threaten me, and by the way don't jump off anything." But they insist if he doesn't do the deed with all twelve of them, or one of them at least, they are definitely going to jump. And so Bors says, "Well that's up to you." So they did. All twelve of them jumped! They were virgin witches, but really. So everyone was just running around looking for their best shields and praying like it was Christmas and I found Bors and asked him—"What's up man?" And Bors was like, "Jesus, Gaheris, we're going to find the Cup of Christ!"

And you know how that turned out. We all nearly died, some of us did die, and we found the blessed thing, Bors and Galahad and Percival did anyway. It's in a bank in Hereford at the moment, not that anyone cares about cups anymore.

Anyway, this time was like that—lots of meetings, the big man looking very serious, everyone looking very serious, I guess I drifted off, and when I tuned back in everyone was looking—just—stunned. As soon as I could I found Bors.

"Bors! Bors! What's the deal?"

2. The Men in the Cave

He puts his arm arm around my shoulder and he says, "Oh, Garry, it's the big one."

"What, bigger than the Grail?" And he looks so sad.

"We've got to take a break."

"How long for?"

"No one knows, could be a thousand years."

"Great! We're retiring? We're done, no more fighting? No quests?"

And he said, "Not quite. We've got to wait, all of us together, until great danger threatens the Isles of Britain, and then we'll awake."

"We're going to sleep?"

"Yes."

"Where?"

And he says, "Well, there's this cave. In Wales..."

It was the strangest journey. Everywhere we went, the whole way, everyone came out to see us–food, presents, blessings, it was amazing. Women, kids, really old people, all the men from farmers to barons, they came out and they bowed or knelt for the big man, and they prayed for us and cheered. They say a lot of stuff about the big man but when you look at what he did, and what we did, I guess–it was something. The Isles of Britain united and peaceful, under a great leader. You foreswore greed and lies, devoted yourself to service, did the job with a smile. Everybody was fine. Easy.

We discussed it and we reckoned that if we had to sleep in a cave for the rest of time, if that was the last mission, it was worth it for the people of the British Isles. Anyhow, I like sleeping. I have great dreams.

Bors was a bit depressed. That guy lives for action. I tried to cheer him up. I said, "Bors, we're going to have the best sleep ever. And with the stuff you've done you're going to have the best dreams. Do you a deal–when we wake up I'll tell you all of them, all the weird stuff, and you have to tell me yours."

He said, "Garry, if we get out of this one we'll be going into the biggest fight in history, but I'll be sure to tell you the best bits if there's time."

So it was a great trip but by the time we got within sight of Craig y Ddinas, at the head of the Vale of Neath, everyone was very quiet. Just the horses stamping in the frost and shaking their manes, and there's the Number One Hippy, Old Merlo, and there's the cave. Merlo said he would look after the horses.

We went in. It was dry at least. We all shook hands, hugged each other, Arthur said, "Men, you've been brilliant. You deserve a rest. You're the best ever. The stuff you've done they'll still be talking about a thousand years from now. And if we have to get up and sort things out again–well, I hope we don't, but if we do it will be worth it to ride out with you again. God rest you, and may flights of angels watch over you in your peace."

Some of us were pretty emotional. We all hugged and then we picked our spots and lay down. It was weird. I was frightened. I thought, wait, this is like–dying or something, and I have this sort of twitch? I go for my sword when I get scared, it's automatic, but Bors was right there and he put his hand on my arm and he smiled at me and he said, "Don't worry, Gaheris. We can do this, right?"

I don't know what I'd have done if it hadn't been for Bors. And then Merlo stepped up and said, "Look, don't anyone worry about this, it's the sweetest sleep, the Sleep of the Just.

You just think calm thoughts, I'll chant a bit and you're dreaming. OK? And if–when–great danger comes, you'll all wake up, you'll feel great, I'll be here, tell you what's going on and we'll take it from there. OK? Alright. Calm thoughts now. Good night everyone, and God bless you."

Someone made a joke then about what Gawain would be thinking about, and he said, "Well it's not Green Men, I can promise you that!" and someone made a crack about Launcelot and who he would be thinking about, and my uncle, and then everyone was dying laughing and it took Merlo a minute to restore order, and we all relaxed, and then it went quiet. Really quiet.

The thing is–that's when it happened. No twitch, nothing– just this overwhelming feeling of certainty, like when I killed the dragons–just, like, *do it now*. I jumped up and ran for it. It wasn't just dying a virgin, sleeping a virgin, same difference. It was–life! I was the youngest! Why did I have to be there? Everyone else was just chilling, thinking about woods or banquets or their favourite horse or whatever and I was thinking about being a knight, and not having–well, not getting to the marrying the lady stage, I mean, lots of rescuing maidens but still a maiden myself, in that way, and this half-Irish maiden I knew, wishing she was there, and then I was *really* wishing she was there. It was too soon to go to bed without ever having been to bed with anyone.

And they woke up–Bors did, and one or two others. We had a row. I was really like–get out of my way man, I'm way too young for this, I don't want to go to sleep or die or whatever it is, I want to have my life, I've never even really kissed anyone, don't try stopping me.

So then there was a fight. We weren't really trying to hurt each other, it was all with the flat of the blades, but the guys– you know, they really take everything my uncle says so seriously, so–I mean, I went berserk, shouting let me go, let me go, but they didn't, about four of them sat on me.

Merlo looked a bit worried, and he had to do the spell again, and that was it, everyone must have fallen asleep, and I was out of it too.

Next thing I know I'm wide awake. And there's this guy, this weird, tall, skinny guy in bizarre clothes, and he's got a pot of gold–we always take plenty of cash on campaigns, so there was loads of it lying about. He looked terrified. I could see straight away this was nothing to do with the great danger–everyone else was still asleep and this guy was obviously a thief. So I drew my sword and I was about to split his gizzard when he took off. No way could I catch him without a horse. You ever tried running in armour? Didn't know what to do then. Couldn't leave the guys. Didn't want to go wandering about without them. Really, really wanted to have a look around though. It must have been a long time since we dropped off, judging by the thief. A whole mad different world out there! Imagine! People in bizarre clothes. What would the women and maidens look like?

So I crept up to the mouth of the cave and there was the stone the Number One Hippy had rolled across it and there was a gap where the thief had got in and out and I edged through, just my head and shoulders.

First damn thing I saw was a dragon. Way high up, flying over dead straight, rumbling, leaving two streaks of smoke behind him in a line. There were other streaks up there too–

must be a lot of dragons. But they were very high so I guess there was some agreement, dragons stick to the sky. Because the farms looked fine, none of them pillaged or on fire, and the fields had got big–huge!–so they must be doing well. A lot of the forest had gone. That was weird. Chopped down a long time ago by the look of it and the stumps dug out. The farms were like small castles, all in stone, and the tracks between them wide, and there were roads which had been paved black, and poles with ropes on top of them linking the farms like rigging on a ship, and lots of cattle and some horses, and loads of sheep. And I looked at it all and thought, yeah, it is a peaceful land, prosperous and quiet. It all came true. He did it! We did it. There is peace and no great danger, and so I went back in and rolled the stone back into place. It took me ages to get back to sleep.

Once Upon A Time in Wye Valley

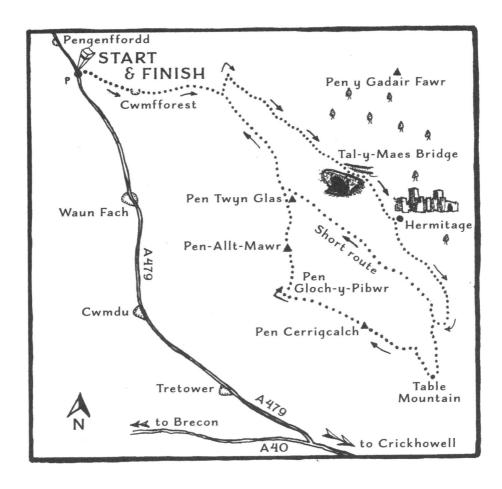

THREE

Once Upon A Time in Wye Valley

ON the occasion of his proposal of marriage my husband's speech to me was, I daresay, one of the most singular a woman ever heard from a man. We were walking by the Wye, which was in a green spate. A great house came into view, its windows reflecting silver winter light.

John Macnamara stopped and said, "That is Llangoed Hall. Edward Williams has it but I will buy it from him and there we will live. Will it suit you?"

I laughed and replied, "It will, very well–but will we be married or scandalously eloped?"

John had recently been much in the gossip in London for fighting with a mob while he was escorting the Prime Minister. John was seldom out of the gossip in London, but now he looked at me with intensity, sank down to one knee, took my hands in his and began to speak.

"Mary," he said, "you see before you one of the greatest sinners of the world. I never go to church. I do go to the

Hellfire Club. I never pray or give to the poor. I have been with many women. You will not know them but I could name them all, and they number 37–wives, virgins, a nun and two sisters among them: I have been an astounding fornicator.

I have fought eight duels and won all of them, wounding six men and grievously maiming two more, sometimes in the defence of my honour, but more often in salve of my pride.

There is not a liquor in Britain I have not drunk to the dregs and I have laid waste to inns, taverns and one apothecary shop while in drink.

The Bible is almost a foreign text to me but I have made a great study of the *Devil's Picture Book*. The familiarity I have achieved thereby has allowed me a skill at cards with which I have amassed some fortune, and you know I have Chilton Park and its estate in Wiltshire; with sensible investments in the West Indies and hard work in England I will in four years have enough to buy the Hall twice over.

Oh Mary, I can only offer myself to you as I am and will be: I do not ask you to accept what I have been. But I will swear to go no more to women, to fight no more duels, to give up gaming and street battling, to turn from cards altogether, to love you and cherish you and furnish you with every ease, happiness and stimulation as may be in my power, to be a true husband to you, and a noble father to our children.

There is no thing on earth I love as I love you. You hold my life and all my hopes in your hands. Will you love me, and marry me, and live with me, until the grave shall rest us, and heaven take you, and the other place, perhaps, have me? If you cannot accept I will understand, but my life will be an enduring winter, and Hell hold no fear for me. Will you marry me, Mary?"

I do not believe a woman with blood in her veins could have refused him. When you hear truth you know it, as I knew it then. My father objected, of course, and so we waited until he passed on before we travelled to Gretna Green and made our vows. Within four years we had four children and the Hall. No one believed that John would change his nature–and perhaps he did not, but he did change his deeds, maintaining only his mighty energies.

Instead of dueling he took up litigation, and was fearsomely successful. He never played cards again. He would sometimes drink but no more than was decent, except on rare occasion. There were no more whores, wives, nuns or virgins. One he had known, Charlotte H-, who was cast out by her husband and left with nothing–he having discovered she had known John before him through her diary (commit nothing to paper that you would not have read by all the world!)–came begging to John in despair and disgrace.

John cared for her as much as he loathed the man and so it was his pleasure to install her in a property he had completed on a high hill at Grwyne Fechan–the Hermitage. It was a remote place John had intended to let or sell to a gentleman. None wanted it, and so he had a road built across the mountains and let Charlotte live there, charging her nothing.

It was widely speculated that she was his mistress, and "Macnamara's Road" a highway to her bed, but neither John or I were troubled by the slanders, "She was once" being too complicated a formula for provincial tongues, who naturally found "She is" much easier.

Only one scandal hurt us in all our happy years at the Hall, when Mary, our daughter, ran away with her brother Arthur's tutor. John sank very low, saying he had fallen from the summit of felicity to the lowest point of misery. It took many discussions and reminders of his own transmutation, from wild blade to matchless husband to bring him to the rueful view that Mary was a Macnamara too, and would one day come good.

"Who are we, John, to disbelieve in redemption?" I asked him, and he laughed at last.

That scandal aside, John only had one regret, which was that he was never successful in joining Mr. Pitt in Parliament, for they were great friends and John would have been a mighty support to the Prime Minister.

He made a happy man, in his later years. A young person came to see him with the idea of making a biography of John's life—a project never completed. This person asked John if there was a secret to his many successes. John answered: "Reputation! When they heard that I had had the hearts of beautiful women, women were intrigued to meet me. When they knew I fought duels eagerly my opponents felt feeble in their arms before I raised my sword. When they knew I cared not for loss or gain, card players folded their hands. And when they knew I would die before I would settle their suits, plaintiffs wilted. Not even death can undermine reputation–time only hardens and extends it. You will see. When I am gone I will be thought larger, wilder, greater and more dangerous than any man could ever be. Only be sure that I am buried like a Viking with my best horse and hound, and in the most spacious grave in Wales!"

And then that old man winked at me, and took my arm, and we went in for tea.

Pop-the-corks Longo, an Italian in Wales

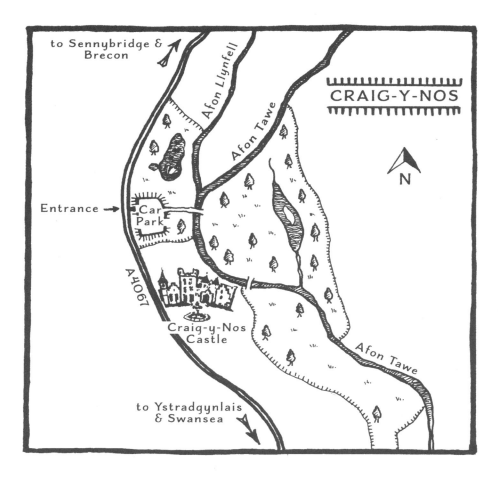

to Sennybridge &
Brecon

Afon Llynfell

Afon Tawe

CRAIG-Y-NOS

N

Entrance →

Car
Park

A4067

Craig-y-Nos
Castle

Afon Tawe

to Ystradgynlais
& Swansea

FOUR

Pop-the-corks Longo, an Italian in Wales

It was this horrible decision–do you want to work for the most famous soprano in the world, this great star, this woman celebrated in London, New York and Milano for her voice, for her performances for kings and queens, for her fortune–you know she used to ask five thousand dollars in gold to be paid before she took the stage?–famous for her love affairs, for her adulteries, for her magnificent treatment of everyone, and the word was she was a perfect employer, you know, she treated dukes and footmen just the same, she only saw people–do you?

Si! Certo! But do you want to work in Wales? What? Where? Oh no, no, no, this place! Dio carne, the first time I saw Wales it was terrible! All these mines, these low down hills, these small people in the rain, I could not understand them, the worst food–I mean the worst food, like it would kill a dog.

Mist, smoke, fires from the furnaces at night, smoke in the day, like the devil's factory, the whole country. I thought 'So this is hell, I have come to hell.' But then the station and the road she had rebuilt and her castle, Craig-y-Nos, and Signora Adelina Patti, the greatest singer in the world came down to meet me as if I was an honourable famous guest, not Longo Giacomo, her new butler.

It was the best decision you can ever make. To be a butler is a special life if you work in a magnificent household, if your employer is good and has a true sense of what is the meaning of life. Signora Adelina knew that meaning from the day she was born in Madrid in 1843.

She held herself like a Spanish woman, you know, like fire and grace, but her parents were Italians, her mother a Prima Donna and her father a tenor from Sicily. She was singing in New York when she was eight. Her first tour–$20,000 dollars. Can you imagine? She sang for Queen Victoria, she conquered Covent Garden, she conquered Europe, she married a French idiot, Henri, Marquis de Caux, who wanted her money. He had other women, she had other men, they divorced, and she is singing Aida when she falls in love with Ernesto Nicolini, a great man, a French tenor who is singing Ramades. They say this was the most passionate performance! He is married but they don't care. He has had many lovers, she has had many lovers. When you are great stars you live and love how you want. They tour Europe together, everywhere they go you cannot get tickets. In Italy, Verdi himself says she is an artist so perfect there has never been her equal. This is true.

The world belongs to her and because she is an artist with a wild heart she has this crazy idea she will live in Wales! And Signor Ernesto wants to shoot and fish in the country. So she buys Craig-y-Nos. And she has made the Winter Garden, the aviary, the new lakes, the clock tower, the stable block, the coach house, the laundry, the whole new wing with twelve bedrooms, dressing rooms, the chapel with stained glass, the generating room for making electric light, the gasometer, and this machine which can make one tonne of ice. For us she makes eight new bedrooms for the servants and they were large rooms, beautiful. And then she makes the theatre! The theatre is magnificent. Blue and gold and cream, like a dream.

The whole stage and all the seats can be raised. There is space for one hundred and fifty. It can be a ballroom or an opera house. The paintings, the friezes, the velvet, the light–this is an enchantment. And in the gardens my friend Con Hibbert makes miracles. There are melon pits, tomato houses, a coleus house, houses for carnations, there is a vinery and muscat grapes so thick you hardly can carry the bunches. He transports huge trees to the grounds, great pines, because Signora Adelina knows the smell is good for her voice. Con Hibbert is a great man. Signora Adelina has great skill in finding the best people, artists like herself, in all the different kinds of life. She found Adamo Adami in Dublin. Adamo is from Stresa, an Italian like me. She employs many Italians because we have the same heart and eye for life like her. Adamo has been working in the Casino in Nice before Signora Adelina dines at the Sackfield Hotel in Dublin. This woman has eaten some of the best food in the world but when she tastes this she asks to meet the chef like she was meeting a prince, Adamo said, and he came to Craig-y-Nos.

And now we are ready for the great parties. The first was

the wedding of Signora Adelina and Signor Ernesto. Maybe there have been weddings in New York or Roma like this but in Wales I don't think so, never. In the glass Winter Garden they have a great feast, and in the great hall another feast for all the workers and servants and people living near! Can you imagine? So many tonnes of meat and vegetables and bread and wagons and wagons of beer. There came letters from the Prince of Wales, the Queen of Belgium, the Queen of Romania, from all these dukes and duchesses and bankers. This is in 1886.

In 1891, with all the works on the castle and the theatre completed, she has the party for the opening of the theatre. It is even bigger than the wedding. The trains came all day–all day! Special trains to carry all the people. Peers of the Realm, Knights, Marquises, Counts, famous opera singers, journalists from New York, Roma, Paris, Havana.

The clothes of the important guests were beautiful, but when Signora Adelina comes on the stage in pink satin and diamonds, so many diamonds, you know there is one star there, one true great star for all time. She and Signor Ernesto sing Act 1 from *La Traviata* and Act 3 from *Faust*. All the servants were listening behind the stage. That night we heard the music of God. It was like the holy spirit in her voice. It was the sensation of my life. And there were 450 bottles of champagne drunk that night, like water compared to that singing.

In the years later some of the performances of the age were sung in this little theatre, in this little country of rain. Signora Adelina believed this—that you must make art where you are, for the place that you are in. When there were no guests we had the special evenings, when she sang and danced with the staff—with us, her servants. And she would always say, 'Pop the corks, Longo!', and so this became my name, because she took champagne with us, and also with the Crown Prince of Sweden and Prince Henry of Battenberg when they came. She saw only people, not titles. And when her time came she left us our memories, and this castle, Craig-y-Nos, for this country of Wales to remember her by.

The Wild Boar Chase

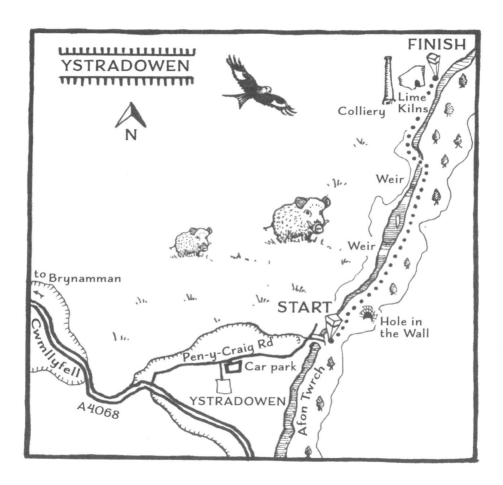

FIVE

The Wild Boar Chase

Have you ever seen a group of people sense threat? Something spreads though them like a shiver. The group is more intuitive than the individual, if less decisive. When I started at the Daily Wales I assumed they'd have the internet, which came in when I was at university, but when I asked how you logged on they looked frightened and said if I wanted to know anything there was the cuttings library. The office was all smoking, so the whole room was a stinking mist swimming with beery sexism you wouldn't believe now–I'd just started, so they called me 'Newsbird'. The computers were weird things on metal stalks like something out of Flash Gordon, green flickering screens and strings of keyboard commands you had to learn because there was no mouse. The editor was a small, terrifying man everyone called Giant Jim, who seemed turbulent with internal violence. The news editor, my boss, known as Tiny Andy, lived on the verge of rage. They ruled the lines of sub-editors, reporters, feature writers, specialists, section editors, their teams and the whole empire of the sports pages. And the internet swept them all away. It's a hotel and apartment complex now, the site where the building stood. What remains of the paper comes out of a building they put up on what used to be the carpark. The interesting thing was the way the internet did for them all. It fed off something which came from them, which was already beginning to rule those old newsrooms when I started, and which has almost wrecked the world now.

"Newsbird! Conference!"

We gathered in Giant Jim's office. Tiny Andy gave the orders.

"The County Echo, Fishguard's finest, did a piece about two wild boars which escaped from a lorry. They were coming from Ireland on their way to a menu. We've had twenty calls this morning from readers wanting to know if they've been caught, if they're OK, if they're dangerous. Some lunatic has offered to buy them and give them sanctuary. It's on the wires, the London papers are after it–my mate on the Mirror says the train from Paddington is full of hacks. Far as I'm concerned, these pigs are on the run in Wales, we're the national newspaper of Wales, this is our story. The splash is Daily Wales Scoops the World–pictures of these pigs, full interview, and then a picture of them being handed over to this nutter to spend the rest of their lives in clover. Got it? Bigger than Chernobyl. Nick, you're on it, Newsbird, you're on it, Marcus is your snapper, Dangerous Dave can drive you. What are we going to call them?"

"Twrch and Trwyth," I said.

"What?"

"From the Mabinogion. Wild boar that laid waste to Ireland. They swam over and King Arthur chased them through Wales until they were all killed. The biggest, the Twrch, ran into the sea off Cornwall."

"Not just a pretty face! Right, Nick the Quick, you're King Arthur, Newsbird, you can be Guinevere. Martin, you get that story of the Twrch ready for the last edition today. Ancient Myth Boars Ravage Wales. Newsbird, keep phoning in, we want the whole chase. Go get 'em. Bring home the bacon."

"Or don't bloody come back," said Giant Jim.

Twrch and Trwyth had been seen on the Preseli mountain. Dangerous Dave kept the car above a hundred on the M4, Nick the Quick ate Wotsits and smoked, Marcus fell asleep on his camera bag. World Joins Boar Hunt was the first piece I phoned in. The farmer who had last seen them was pinned to his front door by cameras; his yard was full of TV trucks; one of the tabloids had hired a helicopter; there were French and Japanese reporters interviewing his kids and neighbours. I had never seen a full media storm before. It was insane. And then it started to get weird.

The boars were seen at Whitland, then on the Black Mountain. We got close enough for Marcus to get a picture. Someone from the Western Mail almost got a loop of rope over one of them and it charged him. The RSPCA shot a bunch of tranquiliser darts at them which all bounced off–very thick-skinned, those pigs. 'Bulletproof Boars', The Sun called them. The tabloids were rabid now. One reporter bought some pigs' trotters from a butcher and used them to make tracks for her rivals to follow. They all had bags of nuts to tempt the quarry, as if wild boar might suddenly start behaving like Labradors.

That night we were put up in a B&B. Nick had a bottle of whisky. I was having doubts about my new profession.

"Helicopters. Satellite trucks. The Iranians and the Iraqis are gassing each other. Why aren't they covering that?"

"It's not news. Five hundred people you've never heard of aren't news. One you have is."

"But wild boar!"

"Animal stories, birds with their knockers out, drunken celebrities–that's money. It's all about the reptile brain. Anything that makes you think dirty bastard, naughty slag, cute kitty–that sells. You're selling a little hit of dopamine in the reptile brain."

Later, in a tiny cold bed reading up on the Twrch, I saw it. Preseli, Whitland, Black Mountain. I had to read it a few times and tell my reflection in the mirror that I wasn't mad. Then I woke Nick.

He read it a couple of times too. "Are you telling me these pigs are following the same route as the boar in the myth?"

"No, the Mabinogion is telling you!"

"Coincidence."

"Three in a row?"

"Bollocks, definitely," he said, but he woke Marcus and Dangerous Dave. We headed for the Amman Valley, the next place in the myth, just in case.

A sodden dawn, the bracken and the grass all sopping with dew and rain, the sky over the valley a boiling grey cloud, and the two black shapes coming up out of the trees. They had a mass, like a dark weight from an older time. Nick, who had a catching pole with a loop of rope on the end and dreams of a job on a tabloid, ambushed them. He got the loop over one and it charged him and Dangerous Dave. There was a wild struggle and Marcus got some great shots of the boar dragging Nick and Dave up the hill, and the other boar coming back to help its mate, and Nick and Dave screaming and running back down. The pigs fled up the valley, one of them trailing the catching pole, and I phoned in my best piece yet–Arthur and Knight in Boar Battle–World Exclusive By Guinevere, as Tiny Andy ran it. The Daily Wales circulation was up across every edition, he said, subscriptions were up, we were making our names.

They went over the tops to Llyn y Fan Fawr, which is definitely the eeriest place in Wales, a cliff plunging down to a lake of dark stillness, a falcon screaming, mobbed by crows, the feeling of nothing changed since the last ice age. We caught up with them again, but this time the one with the pole looped around it actually charged us and gave Dangerous Dave a slash in his left calf. "They're evil! It was trying to kill me!" he cried, as he was carted off to hospital.

Tiny Andy was delighted. "Just what you want at this stage of the story, plucky heroes turn psychotic killers," he said.

Now Wales and the world was divided between Twrch fans, who thought they deserved their freedom, and Twrch haters, who wanted them with apple sauce. I convinced Nick we shouldn't let on about the 'coincidence' of the route because it was keeping us ahead of the pack. When we'd caught them we could reveal how we had done it. By now the rest of the papers had decided I had some special hotline to the prey–Guinevere the Boar Whisperer was born, and I was doing phone interviews with radio stations and being chased by cameramen.

The Mail offered me a lot of money to defect to them, but I wasn't going to be bought, not yet.

The showdown came near Talgarth, in the country of the Ystrad Yw, as the Mabinogion calls it. A small wood, a ring of hacks, who had now started following us, Nick the Quick and Marcus, two guys from the RSPCA with dart guns, and the boars. We got one. Tiny Andy had sent two rough boys from Brecon Rugby Club to help secure the captives, which he had purchased from their Irish owners for an undisclosed fortune. Twrch got away again and Trwyth was slung in the back of a Landrover by the rugby boys. We got away and hid the boar in a pen on a farm near Eywas Harold. Before it had even woken up Nick had filed his exclusive interview, in which Trwyth revealed how he and his mate had come to take revenge on the descendants of King Arthur in Wales, and that they deemed only Guinevere and Sir Nick worthy of capturing them. The nutter turned up with a horsebox and Marcus got a shot of Trwyth sweetly sleeping in a pile of straw, on his way to the pastures of rest. We set off after the other.

Now the papers split, and the country with them. The Sun

ran a piece with a picture of Dangerous Dave in hospital and the gash on his leg blown up to cover half a page–Army Hunt Killer Boar. The Express, The Times and the Mail howled for the destruction of Trwyth and the shooting of Twrch. The Independent kept an animal rights line, and The Guardian, after much vacillation, thought a cautious capture and a resumed journey to the abattoir would be best. Only the Daily Wales, stoking flickering nationalist sentiment, kept the heroic escapees line–and technically they were our boar, the mascots of the paper of Wales, Trwyth as fierce as a Welsh scrum, Twrch as elusive as our fly-half. The right-wing press hired their own gunmen. Vigilantes with shotguns scoured the hills. Mail readers stopped taking their children to school.

"It's madness," I said to Nick, "we've created madness."

"We've created anger, fear and righteous indignation," he said, "that's the first step to power. Bonuses, promotion and prizes next, you wait. You ought to do more TV. You could do anything then–become an MP!"

The end came on the Gwent Levels, near where the M4 lifts up towards the bridge. South of the road, towards the sea, is a still miraculous country of creeks, water meadows and tidal flats. The myth has Twrch fighting Arthur at Llyn Lliwan, which seems to have been a mystical lake or a flooded plain near Caldicott. We were in the right area on the evening when the call came.

There was the boar, plunging through mud and water, racing across the marsh grass. Behind him were men with dogs, men with rifles and tranquiliser guns, men with shotguns, photographers, journalists and a crowd of readers, a ragged hunt baying and yelling, getting in each other's way, out for blood and copy, which they call 'content' nowadays. The shots and darts missed. The photographs show Twrch plunging into the sea and swimming out into the waves until he disappeared. No one saw him go under; he was lost to sight in the greys of tide and twilight. I was glad they did not get him, glad that his end was unknown.

Marcus drove us back to the office and the front page was held while Nick did the full-drama piece of Twrch's last flight, and I completed my great big 'backgrounder', telling the story of how the boar's flight had accorded exactly with the

Mabinogion tale. When it was done I pressed send. It came up on Tiny Andy's screen. He read it. He called me over.

"OK, Gwinny," he said, (I had been promoted from 'Newsbird'), "I'll run it because you've put so much into it and it's too late to find something else. But we'll bury it inside. People don't want to wade through all this stuff, it's too complicated. We're saying that we have just witnessed the re-run of an ancient myth? Save it for the universities and books nobody reads. Death and disaster is what people want."

It was a long time ago, now. But death and disaster is what we gave people, until they lost their sense of hope and history, replaced it with a longing for a glorious past that never was, and exchanged reading for clicking, and feeling for thinking, and news for entertainment, until one day they looked up from their screens and realised death and disaster were all around, and that lies and the appetites of the reptile brain had brought it down upon them.

SIX

Chris and the White Lady

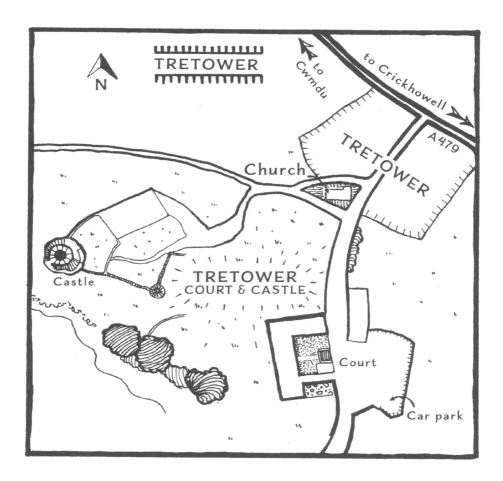

SIX

Chris and the White Lady

IS there a ghost? Maybe. Who's asking? Look, if you wanted to visit Tretower Court between ten and four, Tuesday to Thursday, you had to come and see me and pay. Six quid for adults, sixteen twenty for a family, concessions four twenty. As long as I didn't see you, or if we were closed, you could hop over the gate down the lane and make your own way for free, but you wouldn't get a leaflet. It looked like the easiest job in the world and Mum was on at me to do something so I did it. Easy hours and I quite enjoyed the ride home on the bike–it's downhill most of the way back to town. I thought it was going to be extremely boring, which was fine, I could spend the time messaging Marie and daydreaming, and reading if I felt the need for self-improvement, but I was wrong.

If you have ever studied the kind of people who visit ancient monuments you will have noticed that some of them are more than slightly mad. Not you–I'm sure you're not–but some of them. First day, lady asks me what the birds are called.

There's a flock of geese by the pond sometimes. "Geese, madam," I said.

"Yes, but what are they called?" She was a wobbly looking bird herself with a bit of wattle and eyes you might call beady.

"Their names, you mean?"

"Yes, yes, what are they called?"

"Well," I said, "there's Cedric, Roderic, Alaric, Constantine, Jez, Patroclus, Lepidus, Jim, Hephaestus, Hero, Norm, Ankor Wat, John, Paul, Ringo, George, Divina, Marshall Mathers the Third, he's the one with the limp..."

"I mean the breed!"

"Oh, African Geese," I said, "and they're malicious. Don't go in there with them, you'll never come out. They'll mount you–they'll mount your head on a plaque like they did to that poor Korean girl."

There were actually quite a few Koreans that summer. Some of them took pictures of me with their phones, and some got other visitors to take pictures of them with me. I bet that went down a storm in Seoul–"Look, here's us with this git in a hut who charged us six quid for a leaflet we couldn't read."

It's the first thing you see when you land in Korea, a massive photograph of me with these Korean girls in braces, in front of a hut, in the rain.

I should have put a sign up saying 'There Is NO TEA ROOM'. The number of times I got asked where the tea room was.

"Don't tell me it's gone again," I'd say, "where did you last see it?"

I had a school group, little ones who had all been told that if they were good they could have hot chocolate. They all ran around madly screaming, which I guess was what they understood being good to mean. At least they left the nine hundred year-old castle pretty much the way they found it, and at the end the teacher came up and said, "Where's the tea room? I owe this lot thirty hot chocolates."

"We haven't got one."

"Oh terrific, there's going to be a riot now," she said, and just as she was telling them a barn owl flew out of the battlements and muted, I believe is the correct term, right on the head of a little boy called Jack. He took it very well but half the class had hysterics.

Then, one afternoon, gorgeous it was, midsummer, swallows everywhere and a long hot day which I spent outside the hut and smiling, working on my tan, listening to the cricket on my radio and pretending it was 1903, because you really can't tell what time you're in on a day like that in that valley, this woman comes up and says, "Where's this ghost then?"

She was from Birmingham; I love that accent and she was beautiful actually, tall, with her hair cut quite short and big sort of jumpy bright eyes like smart people have sometimes, and I just wanted to hear her talk so I said, "What ghost?"

"The White Lady of Tretower," she said, "the ghost of Margaret Vaughan, who stares out towards Chepstow waiting for her husband to come back. Roger Vaughan."

"Oh dear," I said, "playing away in Chepstow is he?"

"No!" she goes, laughing, "He was beheaded there by Jasper Tudor, and so she waits for him."

"Oh, her!" I said, "Yes, up the corner stairs there, which is second on your left at the top. If you go really quietly you'll see her. If you find yourself in a tiny room with a hole in the floor that's the garderobe, you won't see her in there except first thing in the morning."

So off she goes with her mate, laughing, and I dared myself to ask for her number when she came back–it didn't work out with Marie–and when they came back I did ask and she gave it to me. She said her name was Keeley but she was laughing and I think it was a fib. She must have been 28 or something, too old for me really, but you've got to ask, haven't you? After she'd asked for a refund and I said no, off they went and then it was four o'clock and time for me to close up.

I liked closing up. It was a bit spooky. The swifts screaming and the smell of warm wood and stone and the strong feeling that you could easily be wearing a doublet or whatever and go round the corner and see a woman in a pointy hat tuning a harp or something. Anyway, I went round and when I got to the solar I just put my head inside before I was going to pull the door shut and there she was.

A lady in white. Every hair on my arms stood up, and on my neck, and I got this prickly rush like you wouldn't believe. She was half turned away from me, over by the window, and I could see part of her face. She was beautiful. Old clothes, long white robes, really old, but not tatty or anything, embroidered.

I couldn't speak. I couldn't breathe. I didn't even shut the door. I wasn't scared she was going to hurt me or anything, I didn't feel any kind of threat, but I was in the same room as a ghost and I could see it–see her. I legged it. Got out, locked the big door, trembling, jumped on my bike, went like mad until I got to town, went straight to the Brit and drank three pints.

I texted Keeley after, told her–you'll never guess what I saw in the solar–but she didn't text back. I thought about not going back or asking for a raise or something, danger money, but instead I made sure that I closed up with the last people there and went out with them. No, I don't believe in ghosts, but I did see one, as clear as you see me.

A Mission Station
on the Buffalo River

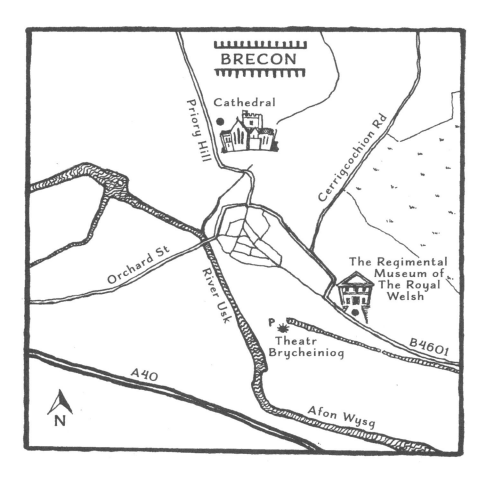

A Mission Station
on the Buffalo River

When I joined the Monmouthshire Militia in 1877 the sergeant said, "Well, John Fielding, if you've been the eldest of nine brothers and sisters you will find the army a natural home, and if your regiment is sent to our colony in the Cape you will find it a fine country, very like the Brecon hills, good ground for cattle and fair-weathered like Gwent on a summer's day. And if you meet any trouble with the Zulus who live there, your new family, the second battalion of the 24th Regiment of Foot, will soon put them in their rightful place, which is under the ground and no cross on top! You will wear the white helmet and the scarlet tunic, you will follow the Queen's colours to the edge of the empire and beyond if so called, and you will carry the Martini-Henry Mark Two, the finest battlefield rifle in the world, with which to send the Queen's enemies to the hereafter at a thousand yards."

And I said, "Yes sergeant, but if my father Michael finds me he will drag me back to Merthyr Road and I will be lucky to see more of the world than Abergavenny." The sergeant took up his pen and wrote John Williams for my name.

"There you are lad, you're a Williams now, one of thirty two in the regiment. Only you and God will know who you were before. Now, you make Him proud."

In January 1879 I was under that great blue Natal sky, sweating in the tunic and itching under the helmet, and after two years I knew the Martini-Henry better than any of my family. I had almost forgotten that I was ever not Private 612, John Williams.

The Mission Station at Rorke's Drift was never supposed to be more than a supply post and hospital, well out of the way, by a ford on the Buffalo river that formed the border of Natal and the Zululand. But then the whole column of Lord Chelmsford's men, 1000 of them, was never supposed to be surprised and slaughtered at Isandlwana.

We had news of that and the 3000 Zulus coming to see us that morning. January is summer in South Africa. I thought that if this was the last day I was going to see it was a sweet one, anyway. I had a pang for the way the mist hangs on the Blorenge at Abergavenny but you can't let yourself dwell like that. In the field, with the enemy on the way, your imagination is not your friend. You lock all those thoughts of home and death and who will make it and who won't deep inside you. You want to be busy, and we were. We built a barricade of mealie sacks all that hot morning. Then I was relieved to be posted to the hospital, out of the sun, to make loop holes in the walls to shoot through, and barricade the windows.

Any solider will tell you the hours before the fight are strange. Your eyes seem to take everything in, every detail and shift in the air, and the day is sharp to you. When the fighting starts time changes too, everything slows right down, so that you seem to see things just before they happen.

We made promises to finish each other off rather than let any be dragged away. Some gave notes for their families or their wives to others. You always wonder who will stop a spear or an old musket ball–the Zulus had some very bad rifles, but still deadly. All that is normal, but that day it did not seem likely that anyone would be left to take the letters home, especially after the detachment which was supporting us fell back. That was the Native Natal Horse, about a hundred of them. They had retreated from Isandlwana without a scratch, but after a short skirmish with the Zulus as they came on the Natal Horse were low on ammunition and could do little more. Another one hundred of the Natal Native Contingent under a Captain Stevenson fled the field, and some of our men who were still left fired after them. I had never seen troops flee a battle before the fight had even started. They were only locals, Natal colonials, but it shook us. I looked around, before we barricaded the hospital door, and there were so few of us. No more than 157 men, they said after, 39 of them in the hospital, and a good few of those too ill to hold a rifle.

There were three or four thousand Zulu coming. You could hear them and see their dust. Not one of us thought we would be alive for nightfall. You get the collywobbles, I can tell you. Your legs shake. Your hands don't seem to grip. You've got something in your stomach like a knot of elvers, all watery and wriggly. You think if you could shout or scream you could clear it, but you can't, so you lock your jaw, keep your eyes front, and try not to think. Mind, we had good officers and stout men. There were no dreamers or panickers; we knew our business and we knew the odds.

So many of them, like a tide they were, with their great white shields in ranks like waves racing in. They came at a flat run. The Zulu spear, the Assegai, isn't meant to be thrown–they're short in the shaft and the blade is very wide, like a fat leaf. It's a slashing and stabbing weapon. Your Zulu's idea is to strike downwards at the torso, stick it in and pull it out. It takes a strong man to do it and if it's you on the end it doesn't matter how strong you are–lungs punctured, guts on the floor, arteries slashed in bundles. And he's a brave man, your Zulu. He will come on and keep coming. Our only luck, though we didn't know it, was that they were led by Prince Dabulamanzi, who fancied a raid after Isandlwana, which he had missed. If it had been King Cetashwayo calling the shots things might have been different. Once Dabulamanzi was committed, even when it didn't go well, he couldn't pull back and lose face. So they came and they came again. Eleven hours of it.

I don't want to say too much about what happened in the hospital. We shot them down until there were piles of them blocking the loop holes and the bullets ran out. We held them with bayonets at the doors. Me and Joe Williams defended one room for an hour until they dragged him out. I smashed holes between the rooms, dragging the wounded through as we were overwhelmed. Henry Hook and I took turns fighting and smashing. It's not something you want to think about much, afterwards, killing men with a bayonet or an Assegai at half an arm's length. You're not really human then, with the roof on fire and the floor a flood of blood.

We fought like rats. We fought like devils. We had nowhere to go and it was as though God looked the other way while we were at it. Breaking holes, dragging men through and killing Zulus, that's what I did at Rorke's Drift. And when it finished, sometime after two in the morning, we had lost the hospital and the barricades, and we had our backs to the storehouse, a small redoubt of mealie bags in front of us and a sea of the dead beyond that like an overspill of Hell.

And afterwards they shipped us to Gibraltar, where the

Governor gave me the Victoria Cross, and then home, and I stayed with the army and married Elizabeth and was in the depot at Brecon during the Great War. We lost our boy at the retreat from Mons. And now I'm old and seeing out my days in Cwmbran. I like a pipe, and I love my nieces, who know nothing of any of this, except that uncle John was a soldier, and they gave him a medal for something he did long ago, somewhere far away.

The medal says 'For Valour' and I think that is right. There was valour in every heart that beat and every one that stopped at the Mission Station of Rorke's Drift. How they chose the eleven they gave it to I don't know. I would have given one to every man, and all the Zulus too. But that is why I was a sergeant, isn't it?

The Real Christmas Day Massacre at Abergavenny

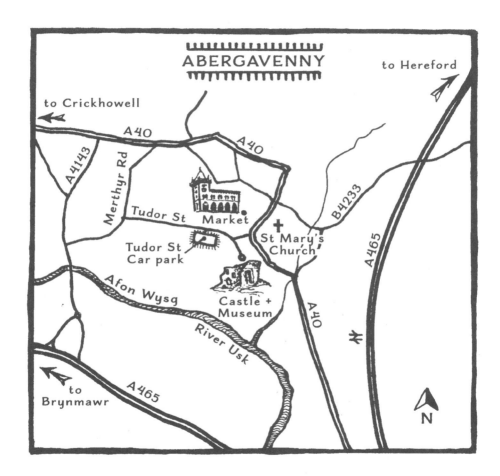

EIGHT

The Real Christmas Day Massacre at Abergavenny

People who don't understand, who only believe liars and
haters, people who have failed to make up their own minds
as to the truth–they call me the Ogre of Abergavenny. Wrong!
They do the typical thing and BLAME. The fact is, my whole
strategy of containment, from the beginning, had been a great
success, a huge success. These were extremely dangerous
people we were dealing with, the Welsh, people who should not
have been allowed back on the battlefield. But that is what the
losers and my enemies wanted!

They wanted me to invite these people to one of my castles,
they wanted me to feed them, they wanted me to donate large
amounts of money and food and ale to these ruthless killers,
because it was Christmas, and when they were done, when
they had taken everything they wanted, wave them goodbye,
maybe give them some presents, give them their weapons, and

just wait around for them to attack us again. Nice! It couldn't happen! I was never going to let that happen.

Let's just remind ourselves of who we were dealing with here. Seisyll ap Dyfnwal was a crooked murderer. In the 1160s he fought Henry Fitzmiles constantly, in all the disgusting ways insurgents fight. My uncle Henry was a good guy, a real good guy. Maybe not so smart as a commander-in-chief, definitely not, but he tried to fight a kind of holding action against Murderer Seisyll and all his men with one hand behind his back. My many enemies would have liked me to fight the same way.

Murderer Seisyll played Henry for such a fool. They made these horrible deals, and then when the deals got broken they fought again, and in the end Seisyll had Henry killed. Maybe Murderer thought that the next guy in the castle at Abergavenny would do the same thing, make a club where people could get together, talk and have a good time. Too bad! The castle was passed to me. Real nice piece of estate, up above the river, but in a terrible state, run down.

First thing I did was build the walls up properly.

Got everyone working and made them do it right, got the Welsh to pay for it with their taxes, and King John in London could see there was some wonderful work going on right away–he was completely supportive of the strategy. HE IS A GREAT GUY! A greatly talented King. He fully supported us when I started a MOVEMENT: Make the Crown Great. I greatly strengthened and expanded our military capabilities. My people cleared forests, drained the swamps, pushed back all the scrub and cover the terrorists had been using to attack the castle. I made sure the soldiers and men at arms were properly equipped and trained. I got some good leaders in there–very impressive people! And you don't hear anyone talking about how I did it all for FAR LESS MONEY than uncle Henry had been spending getting nothing done!

Despite all the distorted and inaccurate gossip, all the scorning and being called terrible names, within a hundred days Abergavenny Castle was a mighty stronghold in the Marches. The civilised world now extended to Abergavenny! We had changed the thinking! And Murderer Seisyll, if he looked at the numbers of soldiers we were getting trained and armed, he would have seen his own were way down. Big trouble. Murderer Seisyll had managed to beat a decent guy who wanted peace, not difficult, but coming up against a real war leader with a vision and a movement, he had no talent. He was going to be out. I devoted ZERO TIME to worrying about how to make peace with terrorists. Did the Welsh ever ask us how we could peacefully co-operate, how they could join the movement or stop opposing it, what they could do to make the roads safe for hard working and wonderful people and travellers? I don't think so! Instead they sat around in the hills trying to figure out how to get rid of me and stop the movement. Sad.

The idea of marching out into the hills, where we didn't control the territory, where we didn't know the ground, where we could be betrayed or ambushed any time was a crazy idea, dangerous. I gathered a team, truly great and talented men, patriots indeed, to plan very smoothly, very effectively and very efficiently how we could defeat the terrorists once and for all, Make the Marches Safe for Civilisation and Make the Crown Great. My agenda was based on a simple core principle. Finishing the Terrorist Threat. As part of this plan I asked my Team for Permanent Change to develop a list of executive actions we could take on Day One of the new year to restore our laws and bring back our security. In fact, we did it even sooner, on Christmas Day 1175.

We realised that we had to fight them on our ground, in our territory. We realised that to do this effectively we needed to separate the terrorists from their weapons. So important. We needed a strategy to protect our people, everyone, and I mean everyone, from surprise attacks and all other forms of attack. And so we decided to invite Murderer Seisyll ap Dyfnwal and his son Geoffrey and all the leading terror chiefs from Powys and their most deadly fighters to a Christmas Day Feast, under a flag of truce, in the castle, where they could eat and drink and discuss co-operation in complete safety. We wanted a lasting peace. They said they did too, but they lied. It went so smoothly. These people were so arrogant and so dangerous they thought they could kill my uncle, then come to my castle and eat out the stores. Bad instincts.

We welcomed them all to the castle. We stacked all their

weapons and their armour in the guard room and locked it. We made sure their servants and their horses had all the food they needed, and then we started the feast. It was a great feast, a truly great feast. They ate goose, venison, pigeons, all kinds of fowls. If I had been sitting in the castle of the man I killed I would not have been so arrogant as to eat so much food I could barely stand, and drink all the mead and beer Murderer Seisyll and his terrorists drank, even if it was Christmas. Lousy leadership.

They drank so much. Then Murderer Siesyll said he wanted to make a speech of thanks and friendship. That was the moment we locked the main doors. And then my security teams burst in wearing full armour, swords drawn. The terrorists fought very hard, they were very dangerous, deadly murderers, who would have slaughtered us if they had the chance. They were extremely violent people. We grabbed every single one of them and gave them the justice they deserved. From the moment they walked in there without their weapons they had lost so badly they just didn't know what to do. Funny to watch, they didn't have a clue! They had treated us with total disdain and disrespect if they thought we could be murdered into submission. But we stayed strong, and we won a great victory, a truly great victory. When you catch a nest of deadly killers like that you cannot afford to be weak. We hunted down Murderer Siesyll's son, Cadwaladr, seven years-old and bound to be a killer like his father, and we gave him justice too.

Because of biased gossip and false reports, and many exaggerations and people saying horrible things, the news of the Christmas Victory did not get the praise it deserved at Court. My many enemies, losers and jealous people, misrepresented the story until King John asked me to move from Abergavenny and take care of business in Hereford. You could tell how successful my strategy was, because my son William foolishly abandoned it, with the result that the Welsh stormed Abergavenny Castle in 1182 and captured William and his wife! That would never have happened if he had listened to me. Bad mistake.

I am William de Braose, and I approved the Christmas Victory 1175, at Abergavenny Castle.

NINE

The True Prince of Wales

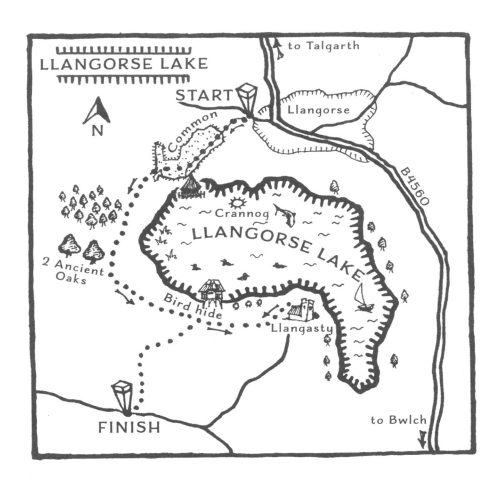

NINE

The True Prince of Wales

Those summers meant coming down from uni, back to Mum's, no money, a job in the Brit or the Bridge, and hanging out with Milo, Fitz and Gruff. Everyone from Brecon to Abergavenny knew Milo and Fitz. When they got their car, 'the General', they became notorious throughout most of Powys. Some sort of Fiesta, 'pimped to the max', bright orange with 'oɪ' on the doors and a Confederate flag on the roof. It cost them a fortune, which I believe they earned through dealing low quality hash and Gruff's online betting system, which actually worked. They loved it so much that when they put it through a hedge and turned it over they spent about six months sticking it back together.

Gruff was the quiet one of the three, thick dark hair and eyes concealing schemes. The brothers called him the Crimelord because when we were children and there was still a garage in Cwmdu, Gruff had got hold of a carton of chocolate which he insisted they sell to kids on the school bus, rather than eat. In those days we spent a lot of time in the barns of his parent's farm, and when we weren't quite kids anymore I spent some time in those barns making them practice their snogging. They gave up too fast: "You're like our sister, Dixie D," Fitz explained, "it doesn't feel right." Around that time I developed a crush on Gruff which has never gone away, but there you are. "Why can't I be Daisy Duke?" I asked all those years ago. "I don't want to be called after her jeep!"

"Because you're always whistling, Dixie," Gruff said. "On about going to uni and moving to London."

"Ambition is critical," I told him, and now I was half way there. Bangor wasn't London, but when I'd got my degree I was going to London, Paris, New York and Berlin, anywhere as long as the lights never dimmed and you could get a haircut after nine in the evening and go to a restaurant after that.

The summer it happened they picked me up at Abergavenny station in the General and Milo got it going about a hundred miles an hour along the bypass, classic Fleetwood Mac on the stereo and all of us howling, "Loving you–isn't the right thing to do…", Fitz building spliffs in the passenger seat and Gruff reclining like a cramped god in his shades next to me. God he was beautiful.

"So how's it going, Dix? Got a boyfriend yet?"

"Two, but they're both too rich and too thick. You?"

"The Crimelord has no time for men or women," Fitz shouted, "he's taking over the internet."

"He's fighting extradition to the United States," said Milo.

"He's perfecting the mind control of greyhounds by remote viewing," Fitz said.

"I'm doing a bit of programming for a Dutch company," Gruff said. "Might be moving to Amsterdam in October."

"You want to marry him quick Dix, Dutch girls," Milo said, helpfully.

"Where are you taking me?"

"Up the Orinoco on the Titanic," shouted Fitz, and cackled.

"Mystery tour, Dix."

"It'll be A and E if you don't slow down."

"The General doesn't have brakes."

"It does, you just don't know where they are."

"Plausible."

Oh, Wales on a summer day! The hills like great hymns against the sky, the sheep dots on the ridges, the buzzards and ravens high up and turning. We'd gone half crazy in those valleys while we were growing up but sometimes there was nowhere in the world more beautiful, and you knew it.

We went through Govilon, Crick and Bwlch as if the police were after us, then Milo took a right and tried to make the General 'get air' over the humps. He played the horn as we passed the Red Lion and took us up the hill, round the corner and down to the water.

"Welcome to the Orinoco."

"It's Llangorse Lake, Fitz."

"Eye of the beholder," he said, handing me his smoke.

"Now behold, the Titanic!"

"We'll drown."

"But at least we'll drown drunk."

Milo loaded a crate of beer into the Canadian canoe, just room for the four of us with it. It was a hot day and I'm a good swimmer.

We set out, the brothers sprawling and drinking in the

middle, Gruff paddling at the back and me at the front.

"Full ahead north!" cried Milo, pointing south. We moved slowly across the water, perfectly happy. At one point we were caught in a current in the middle of the lake. It took us towards the far side. There was a boat moored on the elbow, where a little arm of the lake goes off into reeds.

"Would you say there was an unusual woman in that boat?" Fitz asked his brother.

There was. Tall and red-haired, with a big sunhat, binoculars and notebook.

"Bet she hasn't got beer. Take us alongside," Milo ordered.

"Oh no, leave her be," I said, but Gruff shrugged and grinned and splashed the water with his paddle. "This weird current," he said.

Fitz gave a sort of shriek.

"Something touched my hand–look!"

He had been trailing it in the water. There was a huge half of a fish floating down the side of the canoe.

"Pike!"

"So how big was the one that ate it?"

We came up to the woman in her boat. She looked younger from a distance.

"What're you, the CIA?" was Milo's opening.

"If you're after the Crimelord you can have him, for the reward," said Fitz.

She laughed. She was doing a bird survey, she said, looking for bittern and reed buntings. "But you have to be very quiet," she said, "so it must be break time."

"Beer?" said Gruff.

She thanked him and Milo handed one over, introduced himself as Crockett, Fitz as Tubbs, Gruff as Capone and me as Dixie, as usual. She was a posh sort of woman, hard to age, with a strong face and big slow eyes that really looked at you.

"Are there pikes in here the size of cars?" Milo asked.

"So they say," Julia said. "One ate a bit of a waterskier a few years ago."

"What's with the current?"

"It's an old legend: it won't mingle its waters with the lake because the lake is cursed. It drowned a city of sinners."

"The Prince probably has relatives down there, don't you

Gruff?"

"The Prince?"

"The Prince of Crimelords. Gruff."

"Well, you know about the true prince of Wales and this lake?"

"No."

"If the true prince of Wales comes down to this lake and commands the birds to sing, they will."

"That's me!" Fitz said. He turned round in the boat, knelt up and hollered across the water, "Sing peasants, I command you!"

There were a lot of ducks about and not one quacked.

"Seeing as how I'm older it couldn't really be you, could it?" Milo said. Now he went up on his knees, cupped his hands to his mouth and yelled, "Now hear this, birds! This is Milo, Lord of this land, and he says sing–so SING!"

A buzzard mewed somewhere, fields away.

"Your turn, Gruff," I said.

"I don't believe in royalty," he said, "up the republic. Anyway, it's you. I know it is."

I stood up, the canoe wobbling, and called out. The words

came to me as if I had planned them, though I hadn't. "If I am descended from the great and true princes of Wales then I ask these birds to now declare it! There, proves it's nonsense..."

And right then every single duck, goose and grebe on the lake began to cry out and beat the water with their wings. The noise was unbelievable. Suddenly this wild commotion! Herons, buzzards, stuff in the reeds, swallows in the air, crows in the fields and the waterfowl all went absolutely ballistic. We were just looking at each other, gaping, like, is this the maddest thing ever or are we tripping? Milo clutched his hair. Fitz was turning his head like a loony, as if he was trying to see every bird making a racket. It must have lasted thirty seconds–which is a long time for outright insanity to take hold of a thousand birds at once. Only Julia and Gruff were cool. Julia raised one eyebrow. Gruff kept still, a faint smile on his face. It was a real hullaballoo, and then it stopped.

They all looked at me.

"Dixie, what just happened?" Milo looked dazed.

"Told you she was."

We all looked at Gruff.

9. The True Prince of Wales

Gruff took off his shades.

"Whoops. Bit of a cheat there. Your mum told me you were a princess," he said.

TEN

The Lady of the Lake

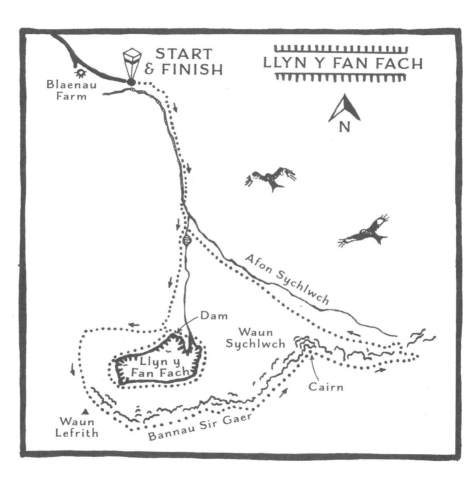

START & FINISH

LLYN Y FAN FACH

N

Blaenau Farm

Afon Sychlwch

Dam

Waun Sychlwch

Llyn y Fan Fach

Cairn

Waun Lefrith

Bannau Sir Gaer

TEN

The Lady of the Lake

I always look at their hands. Hands are what they touch you with. His were quite small, and clean, for a farmer. I could see he had a temper, the more I looked at him, but I thought you can change people or they can change themselves–the best of them can become the way of them, I thought. Fool! I'm never marrying anyone again. It's not a pattern! Guys being idiots is a pattern. And I hate dirty nails, long nails, anything like that, ugly fingers, ugh.

How do I get a guy? It almost gets boring. When you only have to look at someone, and they're like, "Huh! Phwoar!" Raise your eyebrows and sit close to them and they're easy. They can't tell when you're being sarcastic, or they don't care. I don't get it.

I counted the other day. I was going to forget so I wrote them down. Fifty-three. Yeah, I'm not bad, but you know, not that pretty. Oh, stop it! Anyway, can someone please tell me why they always, always mess up? Six months was the longest, before him.

Oh it was a beautiful, beautiful day. Actually hot sun. July. Water almost warmed up. It's never warm, Llyn yr Fan Fach, but it was this blue, blue beautiful day and he took his shirt off, lay on the bank. I studied him and he looked lovely so I came out of the water and sat next to him. I know, right? Same trick. Works every time! Fifty-three times in a row! I'm a water–thing. Nymph, sprite, nereid, whatever–the Lady of the Lake, aren't I?

He was nice looking, really nice looking actually. Said hello, started chatting and he did that thing–you're so beautiful, you're amazing, la la, will you marry me? I did like him. He came up to the lake every day for weeks and he never shut up, going on about love and beauty…

I really liked him. In the end I said if we get married you can never hit me. Right? If you do it's over. Really clearly I said, if you even raise your hand at me, if you even touch me in an unkind way three times it's finished. Swerve it if you can't promise me. If you're not sure. Of course he was sure. Completely sure. Swore on his soul. So we kissed and the way he held me was lovely.

Sometimes I kissed guys who weren't that attractive. There was one guy who'd taken his girlfriend up to the lake, camping–in the morning she's still asleep, he comes down to the shore, I pop out, say hi, and the next thing he goes all wibbly...Yeah, I kissed him! I don't care, it's not me doing it behind someone's back is it?

They were never going to have a chance with someone like me–not being vain–just–honest! And you can see they know it. They can't believe it. And they'll never forget it, it's like you're giving them something amazing. Really amazing. It's good to do that. And if someone tries to kiss you, even if you don't really fancy them–I sometimes think, is it worth the hassle of saying stop it, and them getting all embarrassed? It's just easier to kiss them, you know? It can be.

With him–we just held hands for ages. And then he hugged me for the longest time. That was lovely. That was the best really. He promised he would love me and honour me and in the end I said OK. Yes. I do.

I did kind of like the idea of children and we had great

kids. I got completely into it. Sweetest kids, just the sweetest, kindest–really caring, you know? I don't know where they get it from. They're doctors. They're all physicians. Kind of weird they're going to grow older than me. But I really like little ones. Yeah, I'd have more. If I met someone nice. But I'm not getting married again. I don't know what it is. I can't see any pattern in them except they're men. If you could make one out of a combination of two or three of them you could have the perfect man. Ha! The perfect man...

I thought he was as close as I was going to get, but he started breaking his promise–it's not enough to love someone if you don't honour them. That's the bottom line. I could see what was going to happen, I told him, I told him, and we did try really hard. I really supported him. We went to see a counsellor before he even laid a hand on me the first time because I knew what would happen but–he didn't get it? He could have done. I think he could have done, but he didn't.

The first time he was coming back from work. Marrying me was the best thing he ever did. I told him he would be massively successful and he was. Businessman, buying and selling, all that boring stuff. But he did well, we had a great house, loads of holidays, kids in posh schools, it was fine, you know, fine. But then he got lazy and arrogant and he lost money. He was coming back from meeting his broker one day and they'd lost money and I annoyed him and he hit me. Slapped my face. Not that hard. I told him if he ever did that again it was over. More counselling, for his temper and whatever his problems actually were. There's messed up and then there's messed up, isn't there?

I advised him to keep going to counselling, to get himself sorted out. I mean, everything he tried to do about it helped, even in little ways. He was really successful, great dad, made me happy, happy enough. I don't know what it was. But he didn't do enough about it–people are always telling themselves they can manage. Or he was just an idiot, underneath.

Second time, he shouted at me after a dinner party and I told him to get lost. He slapped my bum. And then tried to make like it was a joke. I said, last time, that was the last time. He realised I was serious and he was gutted, really gutted. That night he washed my feet in the shower and he held on to my legs. Knelt down and held onto my legs and cried and said he was sorry.

The evil part of me was so angry. So angry. I was shaking and I wanted to do something. The same part of me that cheated on other guys, the part of me that had that guy camping with his girl that time, that part of me wanted to do something. Didn't though. I didn't do anything.

And then he did it again. A couple of years later. I hadn't really said anything, just some stupid row. I was playing music really loudly and dancing around, I loved the music then, the 80s, Duran Duran, I played it every day, and I love 90s stuff, Kim Mazelle, it was a good time to be living in your world then. I was doubly gutted when he did it the third time and I had to go back to the lake! And the kids, of course, but I never left them, I used to see them all the time. They think it's weird I've never told them where I live, but anyway. I was really raging–I just said, you know what it means and you do that–you still do that. Goodbye, idiot.

He started crying. The funny thing was the cat, the dog, the horses, even the newts in the pond all followed me when I walked out. It was a big scene, and then when it had quietened down I had to sneak the horses back, and the cat, and the dog. The newts stayed in the lake. And he lost all his money, lost the house, had to move back in with his mum. The kids were at uni doing medicine, all three of them. They've made a name for themselves since–The Physicians of Myddfai–I can't tell you how proud I am. He's getting old now. He never remarried. He wasn't much of a catch by that time. I don't hate him. He loves the children and they love him. It's just a bit sad really. But you can't change anyone, can you? I mean, being with you might make them change, sure, but you can't control how.

Hey, you know that guy in the jacket? He likes you, he's looked over about five times. N-o-o he isn't! No, it's you, definitely.

Yeah, he is quite. Just not my type… something…I don't know….something about his hands maybe. Oh! Whoops! Here we go. You're talking to him, right? I'm with someone. If he tries anything, I'm with someone.

Horatio Clare

Horatio Clare's first book, *Running for the Hills*, an acclaimed account of a Welsh childhood, won the Somerset Maugham Award and saw Horatio shortlisted for the Sunday Times Young Writer of the Year. His subsequent books include *Truant, A Single Swallow, The Prince's Pen* and the best-selling travelogue, *Down to the Sea in Ships*, winner of the Stanford Dolman Travel Book of the Year. Horatio's first book for children, *Aubrey and the Terrible Yoot*, was listed for the Carnegie medal and won the Branford Boase Award 2016. His essays and reviews appear regularly in the national press and on BBC radio.

Jane Matthews

Jane Matthews grew up in Bristol. She previously worked in the film and TV industry as a scenic artist and prop maker, before escaping to the remote Welsh Island of Skomer, where she monitored seals and published her first book, Skomer. She is now based in Shetland, working as an illustrator and exhibition manager. She illustrated her first children's book in 2015, *Aubrey and the Terrible Yoot* by Horatio Clare.